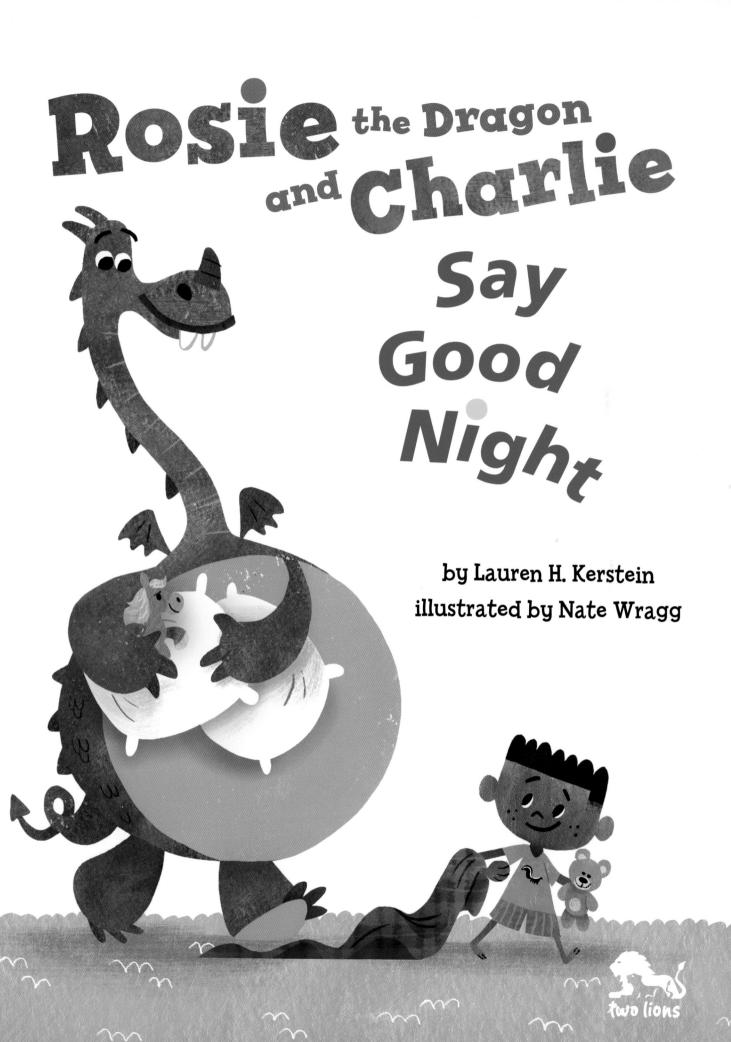

Rosie the Dragon and Charlie Say Good Night

by Lauren H. Kerstein

illustrated by Nate Wragg

two lions

Published by Two Lions, New York

www.apub.com

Amazon, the Amazon logo, and Two Lions are trademarks of Amazon.com, Inc., or its affiliates.

ISBN-13: 9781542018487 (hardcover)
ISBN-10: 154201848X (hardcover)

The illustrations are rendered in digital media.

Book design by Tanya Ross-Hughes
Printed in China

First Edition

10 9 8 7 6 5 4 3 2 1

For S, D, and J. From Goldbug to *Goodnight Moon*, Pookie to Bidgood,
I'll forever cherish our bedtime snuggles.
—L. H. K.

For our little bedtime bean
—N. W.

Oh, hi! I didn't see you there.
I'm Charlie.
This is Rosie, my pet dragon.
We're playing superheroes.

YIKES, Rosie! I can see your tonsils when you yawn! It's time for bed.

Hey, Rosie, where's Vern?

Vern is Rosie's favorite stuffed animal.

Every night he magically disappears before bed.

We search . . .

and search . . .

and search.

We collect a few other essential supplies.

You know what, Rosie? Let's grab the fire extinguisher, just in case . . .

Rosie clutches Vern
and gallops to her room.

☾ Bedtime ☆

1: GATHER SUPPLIES.
Don't forget the fire extinguisher.

2: BATH TIME.
Remember, water belongs
IN the tub!

3: PAJAMAS. ☆
Cool pajamas only. We don't
want any fiery eruptions!

☆

4: BRUSH TEETH.
I'll grab my raincoat!

5: READ.
Books are the best.

6: LIGHTS OUT.
Vern will be right there
with you.

☆

☆

Next up, bath time!

I add Rosie's favorite knight toy and a cup of bubble bath.
No, Rosie, Vern does NOT want to swim.
She snorts and plunges Vern into the water.

Rosie adds lots of toys and way more bubble bath.

Rosie, that's too much!

We race through bathing before the bubbles hit the ceiling and . . . flood the whole floor.

Rosie, it's time to get out of the tub. Now!

See, Rosie, doesn't it feel good to dry off?
Speaking of dry, did you notice Rosie's shedding scales?
She needs lotion (and I need a vacuum).
I rub lotion on Rosie.

Rosie rubs lotion on Vern.
YUCK!

Okay, Rosie, it's pajama time.

I steer Rosie away from footie pajamas since it's not that cold outside, but she yanks out a colorful pair. Plus a matching pair for Vern.

Um, Rosie, you'll overheat. Find something else.

Rosie pretends she doesn't hear me. Thankfully, I'm prepared with a fan.

Last week when she wore footie pajamas
to a sleepover, it was a hot mess.

UH-OH! The fan isn't working.

Let's splash cold water on your face. NOW!

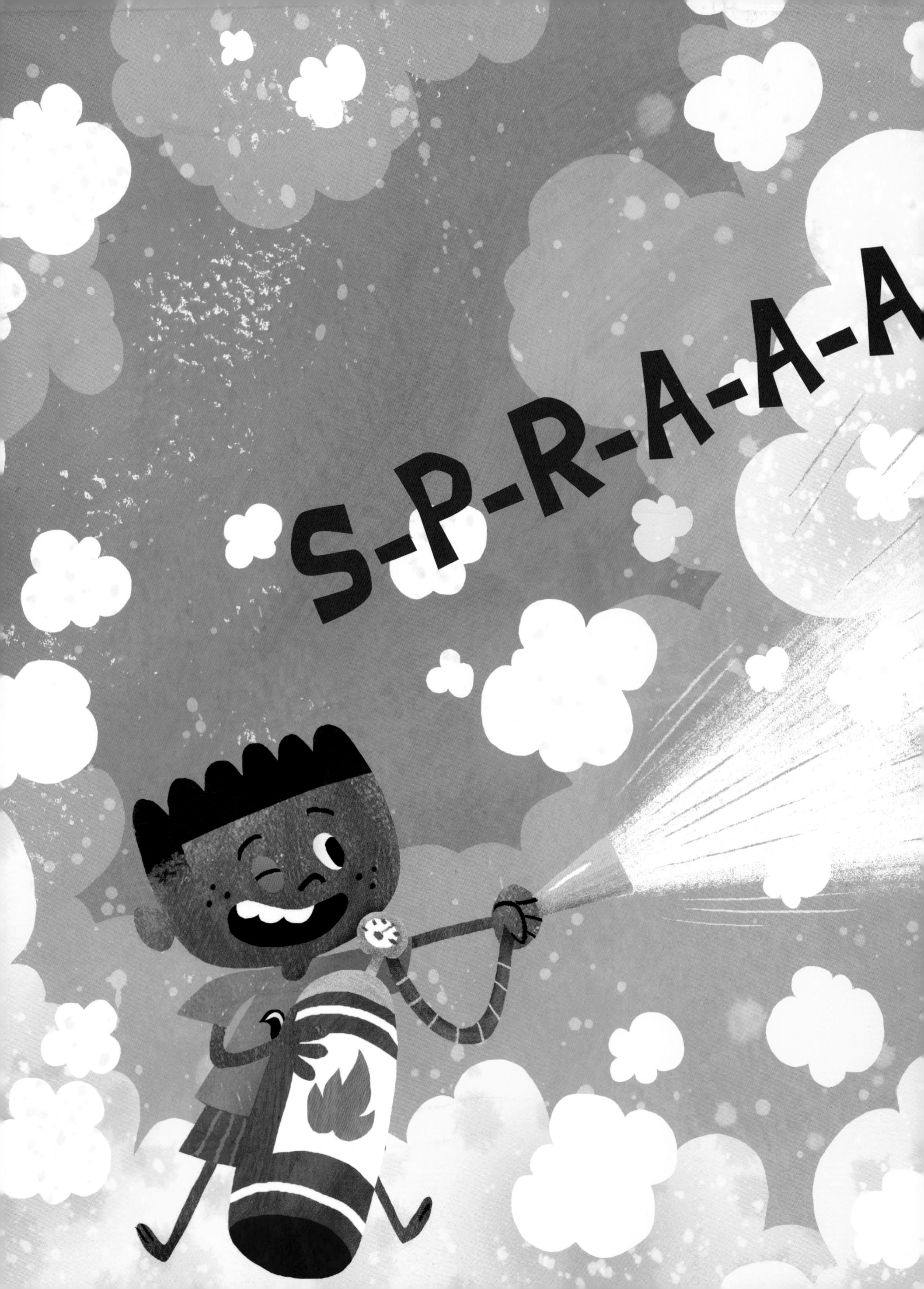
S-P-R-A-A-A

Okay, Rosie, it's time
to brush your teeth.
I pull on my raincoat.

Remember, you just need
a small amount of toothpaste.

Rosie loves brushing her
pearly whites. She scrubs
every single tooth. Twice.

I help Rosie select a few books.

*No, **FEROCIOUS KNIGHTS** is **NOT** a comforting bedtime story. Let's pick another one.*

Next, Rosie turns on her
night-lights. All of them.

Finally, we snuggle
together to read.

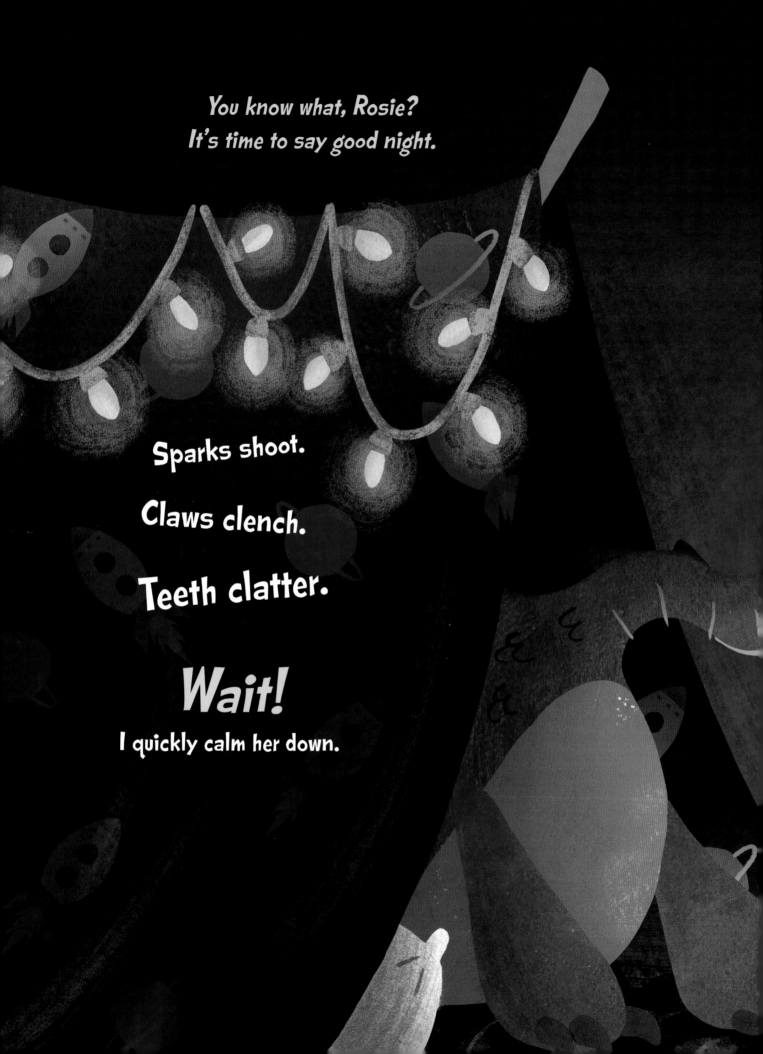

You know what, Rosie?
It's time to say good night.

Sparks shoot.

Claws clench.

Teeth clatter.

Wait!
I quickly calm her down.

I know it's dark outside,
but you have your night-lights.
Vern will keep you company.
Of course you can cuddle
with my shirt while you sleep.
I just need to . . .

Rosie hugs Vern—and a few stuffed animal friends—and closes her eyes.

Terrific! Rosie is sleeping!
I slide into the tub for
a nice bath. Until . . .

R-R-R-RUMBLE!

Oh no! Rosie is petrified
of thunderstorms!

I hop out and bolt
to the bedroom.

FLASH! CRACKLE!

Rosie peeks out of
her tent, panting.

SHRIEK!

Here, Rosie, wear these
while you cuddle with . . .

. . . Uh-oh! Where'd Vern go?

We search . . .

and search . . .

and search.

Hooray!
We found Vern.

Rosie, Vern, and I lie together as the rumbling turns to grumbling, and the storm fades away.

Sweet dreams, Rosie.